The Bremen Town MUSICIANS

written and illustrated by David Johnson

Rabbit Ears Books

10/2005

ABDO Publishing Company is the exclusive school and library distributor of Rabbit Ears Books.

Library bound edition 2005.

Library of Congress Cataloging-in-Publication Data

Johnson, David, 1915 Feb. 18-
  The Bremen town musicians / written and illustrated by David Johnson.
      p. cm.
  "Rabbit Ears books."
  Summary: A retelling of the Grimm tale in which an old donkey, dog, cat, and rooster, no longer wanted by their masters, set out for Bremen to become musicians.
  ISBN 1-59679-222-1
  [1. Fairy tales. 2. Folklore—Germany.] I. Bremer Stadtmusikanten. English. II. Title.

PZ8.J459Br 2005
398.2'0943'0452—dc22
[E]

2004059646

All Rabbit Ears books are reinforced library binding
and manufactured in the United States of America.

ABDO
Publishing Company

he history I am about to tell took place in the latitude of the Germanies, east of the Weser River and west of the Oder, in the age of the Hanseatic League, and so long ago that everything was different and quaint. It was set not in a city or a town or even a country village, but on a small farm, amid fields and pastures and gardens, barns and byres, crops and livestock and farm implements.

The farmer who lived there was practical and hardworking, and his wife, thrifty and modest. They were considering what to do with their aged donkey, who was lame and broken-winded.

At one time the donkey had been the backbone of the farm, carrying the grain and pulling the cart and turning the mill. But no more. The animal was now quite useless, I'm afraid. And his practical master, impatient with the notion of keeping a donkey to live at ease like a gentleman, made plans to put an end to the creature.

Although the donkey may have been aged, he was shrewd. And so one night he lit out of his stall and through the wicket and down the lane, until by dawn he was well along the high road toward Bremen.

At the free city of Bremen, the aged donkey was certain he would find a place in the town band. And why not? He had a musical voice, the character of which was somewhere between that of a snare drum and a saxophone.

Along the way, early that morning, the aged donkey met a morose old dog sitting by the road, scratching his flea bites.

"Hello, friend Dog! You are pulling a long face there. What makes you blue?" said the aged donkey.

"Blue? Who, I? Once I was as vigorous and keen as any spaniel. But I am an old dog now. My master will not suffer me to rest upon my achievements, and my position has been usurped by a young basset hound. So here I am, a fugitive—toothless, homeless, and pointless."

"Well, upon my soul," said the aged donkey. "My tale is little different than yours. Why not come along with me to Bremen? I am on my way there to be a musician."

The dog was easily persuaded. So the newly-made friends set out along the way to Bremen Town. The aged donkey began to sing, and the old blue dog joined in duets, carols, harmonies, and two-part inventions. The dog sang bass.

To get to Bremen Town, you go down the road a way, and then a way further, and then finally you are on your way on the way to Bremen.

Here our companions met a world-worn and out-at-the-elbows cat, sitting all alone, wearing a face as long as a wet fortnight.

"Hello, friend Cat!" said the aged donkey. "You are crying most piteously. Why is it so?"

"I cry, for I am old," said the shaky cat. "And when at last I have derived the methods of mousing, my age has deprived me of the means."

The dog produced a hankie and patted away the tears from the eyes of the forlorn cat.

"Donkey here, and I myself, understand how you must feel."

"Yes, my mistress understood, too, but was not inclined to provide for my retirement. And I understood that my life would be longer the shorter I stayed."

"Yes, I understand well," said the aged donkey. "Ancient though I be, I am on my way to Bremen to perform in the band. And this old blue dog is coming along, too. Our tales are much the same as yours, in a manner of speaking. Pray join us, friend Cat."

"Indeed, yes," insisted the old blue dog.

Thus encouraged, the shaky cat gave an impromptu in a voice like a violin—or maybe it was more like a rusted hinge. The donkey added a singular harmony and the dog sang bass.

And away they all went, down the highway, Bremenward.

They sang along as they went, and just as they were resolving the fugue in "Row, Row, Row Your Boat," an altogether unfamiliar voice stuck in an oar at the part where they all go "Merrily, merrily, merrily, merrily."

"Hello! Mercy! Who is that?" said the old blue dog.

"It was none of us," said the shaky cat.

"We were all occupied, singing merrily," said the aged donkey.

"It was I, the rooster," said a voice from nowhere.

"You, the rooster?" said the shaky cat. "Where?"

"Here I am," said the rooster. And there he was indeed, a cocky rooster, standing bravely atop a milepost.

"You're a saucy fellow," said the aged donkey.

"So it would seem," said the rooster. "The farmer's wife wanted to have me fricasseed and served with a sauce for Sunday dinner, so Saturday night I flew the coop."

"Well, friend, I'm on my way to Bremen Town to be in the band. Old blue dog has joined up, and the shaky cat is coming, too. A quartet is one more than a trio—so come along!"

The rooster was flattered. "Of course, I do have a trained voice," he said.

And the rooster began to sing in a voice that was like a musical saw—or maybe a bagpipe. The donkey recognized the tune and sang along. The cat provided a sweet harmony and the dog sang bass.

And thus they continued along the way to Bremen.

But, you know, Bremen Town is never just around the corner. No, Bremen is usually quite a bit further than you think at the start. And after a while your shoes begin to pinch, maybe your trick knee starts doing tricks, and then pretty soon it gets late in the day. So it was with our travelers, and they realized they would not reach the Philharmonic at Bremen Town that day.

The rooster looked around. "The countryside hereabouts looks uninhabited."

The donkey looked around. "And inhospitable."

The cat looked around. "And unhealthy."

The dog looked around and found a comfortable spot under a nearby tree. There he snugly established himself and was soon fast asleep.

The donkey, impressed with the logic of the dog's position, found himself a billet nearby. The cat, however, was concerned that sleeping on the damp ground would be bad for his rheumatism, and climbed to a limb about halfway up the tree.

The rooster felt that he would be safer the higher he went and flew to the very topmost perch. Before he retired he looked about, and in the near distance he perceived the dim glimmer of a flickering light.

"Friends! I see a light not far away. Let's take a look!"

Flying down from his outlook, the cocky rooster led the old blue dog, the shaky cat, and the aged donkey into the woods. At length they came to a lonely house.

"Shhh! Wait here and I'll see what is afoot inside," said the donkey.

He tiptoed up to the window and peeked in.

There he saw four terrifying and bloodthirsty loathsome thieves. One had scars and a mustache and wore a rakish hat with a jaunty feather. Next to him, with his feet on the table, snored a cossack of rueful countenance, a frizzy beard covering his jaws and the rest of his head otherwise innocent of hair. Then there was his dwarfish brother, the thieves' titular leader, half as tall but twice as mean. And the fourth thief, a veritable giant, sat at the end of the table supping greedily on large helpings of stew.

The table before them groaned with food. Roasts and ragouts and goulashes, fowl and forcemeats, hampers of breads and biscuits and buns, and baskets with every kind of cheese. No vegetables, of course, since these were especially bad criminals, you understand? But there were, however, many sweets: eclairs and napoleons and chocolate cake and pastries of all sorts.

The donkey gazed hungrily upon the food, then at the villains, then at the food again, and still once more at the robbers, deducing from their gruesome appearance that they would most likely be disinclined to share their great feast with his quartet. So he returned to his colleagues and related all that he had seen, with considerable attention to detail.

"Sausages and steaks and chops and bones!" said the old blue dog.

"Cheese and chowder and cream!" said the shaky cat.

"Charlottes and macaroons and chocolate cake!" said the cocky rooster.

"And knives and pistols and cutthroat brigands," said the aged donkey. "But listen here. I have an idea."

The four hungry friends put their heads close together and cooked up a plan. They would serenade the bandits for a bit of supper.

It can't be described exactly how it was managed, but at last the old donkey balanced himself atop a rickety barrel near the window, and the dog pulled himself up on the withers of the donkey, and the cat stood on the back of the dog, and the rooster perched atop the shoulders of the cat.

When they had all stopped wiggling and wobbling, the rooster gave the signal by pulling sharply on the cat's tail. The cat meowed, indicating the key; the dog barked on the downbeat; the donkey began to yodel; and up struck the entire band.

Several measures into the piece, the musicians' enthusiasm undid them, and the barrel upon which they were supported suddenly gave way. The quartet teetered to the right, then corrected itself to the left; then it swayed backward, and finally it hurtled headlong through the window into the parlor with a terrific smash.

With the dog barking, the cat meowing, the donkey braying, and the rooster crying "Cock-a-doodle-doo," the musicians crashed helter-skelter upon the robbers.

When confronted by this cacophony and the harrowing apparition of feathers and fur and claws and hooves, the fierce robbers reacted with panic and confusion.

The midget captain shrieked aloud. The mustachioed rogue goggled in amazement. The bald whiskerando jumped into his boots. The slow witted giant fled out the door, and the others—falling all over themselves—followed him forthwith.

Disappointed by their spoiled debut, our heroes collected themselves and smoothed their fur and straightened their feathers. Then they sat down around the table and addressed the feast: stews and cheeses and pies and casseroles. They ate and ate and ate and ate until they could eat no more.

The aged donkey said, "I'm sated. There is a pile of straw in the yard where I'm going to lie down."

"And, well, there's a rug behind the door where I can curl up and rest," said the old blue dog.

"And there's a cozy corner for me near the hearth," added the shaky cat.

The cocky rooster, considering further discussion superfluous, flew up to the roof beams, snuffed the lamp, and was soon asleep.

It was long after midnight when the robbers dared to return to the vicinity of the house and discuss the possibility of reclaiming their abode.

"All that I remember was the creature's immense size," said the tiny captain. "I'm sure that it was a demon of the most unimaginable sort."

"What I recall was its ghastly hair," said the bald picaroon.

"I was certain it could gobble us up in one bite," said the hungry oaf.

"But it is quiet now," said the fourth, straightening his cap. "Maybe it's asleep."

"Maybe it has left."

"Maybe it was something that we imagined."

"Or maybe it was just something that we ate."

And then the feather-capped bandit, who was always quite brazen, stole back to the house.

Ever so gently the robber pushed open the door. He held his breath and waited for movement inside, but all was still. He silently tiptoed to the hearth and listened closely. Nothing stirred.

The light was dim, so he took a match from his pocket and struck it.

The sudden explosion of light from the match rudely awoke the shaky cat from his slumber. He immediately leaped at the intruder in self-defense, hissing and spitting and scratching, slashing the thief's nose. The robber shrieked in pain and horror and fled for the door.

The old blue dog, who had been sleeping nearby, was startled, and bit the robber so viciously upon the muscle of his calf that his hat flew off.

Holding his hand to his bloodied nose and hopping on his one good leg, the thief blundered through the door into the garden, where he trod upon the donkey.

And as donkeys will, our aged maestro placed a swift kick upon the gluteals of the fleeing villain, who was thereby launched through the garden gate. And even the cocky rooster, incited by the hubbub, crowed from the rooftop in his very loudest voice: "Cock-a-doodle-doo!"

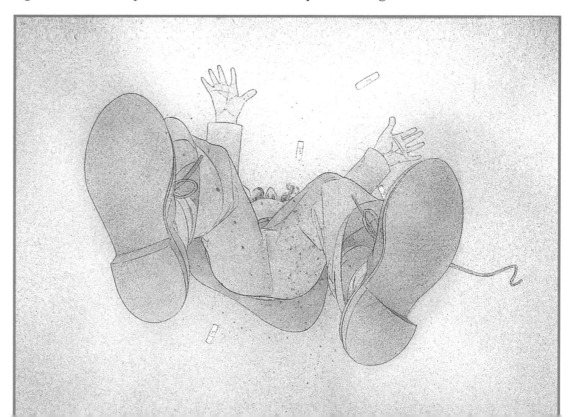

The thief sped like the wind from the yard and into the arms of his companions. "The devil himself holds court there!" he cried. "He cursed me up and down with dreadful epithets. He spit poison on me. He pierced me with his claws. Next to the door stands an unlovely fiend with a hideous spear who stabbed me repeatedly about my body. In the yard is an immense ogre of unnatural strength who belabored me with his club. And upon the roof sat a demon judge, decreeing, 'Bring the rogue to me!'

"It was my soul they wished, so I took to my heels, and nothing will ever take me back to that forsaken house."

The rest of the company, finding the story terribly frightening, renounced their careers as thieves and immigrated to the city-state of Venice, where they formed a troupe of exceptionally adept singing gondoliers.

And so our four heroes were content to remain in their new home, where they rehearsed their musical compositions twice daily.

As for whether the musicians ever continued on to Bremen Town to play in the band, I am not so sure.

Suffice it to say the aged donkey, the old blue dog, the shaky cat, and the cocky rooster lived the rest of their lives in perfect harmony.